Oh Muse! Where the fuck are you!

by pfg powell

Contents

Oh muse, where the fuck are you!

I'll pass

The obvious lines were —
well, just all too obvious,
and did not grab me
sparked nothing but a sigh.
Love? Our children? Pets? Memories?
Petty theft? Ah, now there's a thought:
A petty theft by a homeless woman,
and charity from those
who spot her desperate act
and let her go with her loot
and their best wishes
(and quiet, un-shed tears)?
Er, no. Corny, hackneyed, phoney
bleeding heart stuff ain't my style.
As for wide-eyed, cute
and forlorn puppies
abandoned in a city pound,
and their insistent, yelping pleas
for family? Give me a break!
So, I'll pass, admit that this one's
got me beaten.

Taken? Sad to say
but sorry I'm not moved.
except to sneers and
threadbare cynicism
and that's not what we want, now, is it?

Keep it coming

Mother, Mum, Momma, Mama, Mutter?
Well, there's room for goo now,
isn't there,
lashings of it, a slow squelch
through mawk and careless
self-delusion,
ten, twenty bows to convention
and not one to truth.

Do none of us recall
the thoughtless lack of kindness,
the solipsistic insistences
that her life was of nothing
but to make your bed and
later as a teen
make you feel uncomfortable?

By all means squelch the goo
and call it love and memory
but don't deny yourself
a few other recollections

though by all means keep them
very private and confess to no one,
the shame remaining hidden in
your soul
where none might peek without
your say-so.

But I'll be kind:
she, too, was once young
and thoughtless.
There! Does that help?

Blank. I'll give you blank

A hasty rattle down the lane
ignoring sense or any rhyme
dodging through the rain in France
to beat the clock, arrive on track
leading us a merry jig.
A song sung well without a point
a farmyard pen without a calf
drinking deep in some old bar
getting drunk just for a joke.
Meet a friend who's travelled here
who tells you sadly he's been fired
and drowns his sorrow with a gin
then turns in early cos he's beat
The house is empty, no one's home
so nowhere to escape the sun.
So, not a rhyme in sight or sound
(and even less sense).

Ah, to be wise

When I was young and still unaccustomed
to the cruelties of the world
and idealistic, daft enough
to imagine goodwill
would always conquer evil
I could not understand
the coldness I felt all about
in those older, in those wiser,
in governments, in ideologies
a lack of love, a lack of fellow feeling
so that each new day the world awoke
to discover much all was covered
in a thin layer of wise cynicism
and an habitual and lazy disregard
for the possibilities of grace.

I now know it was — it is — not
always a coldness
but a pragmatic wariness,
a resolution to preserve and protect,
for the good of one's tribe

what can and might be preserved
and protected
though in preserving and protecting
our own interests
the lives of other tribes are
condemned to feel the chill.

I was young then and stupid,
more admirable perhaps, but stupid,
unversed in the ways of the world
and my intellectual progress was
made in baby steps.

Yet still a part of me (as stupid
part perhaps,
my stupidity not yet completely
choked off
by my new wisdoms)
could not help yearning for the world to warm
a little
in its daily round,
unashamedly to recall the stupidity
of its youth, that the day might come
when warmer hearts would glow
and that morning rime of cynicism could no

longer form

day in, day out, week in, week out, year in, year out.

Foolish thought. Stupid me.

They say God works in mysterious ways,
well, they were bloody mysterious
that day,
and one hundred and sixteen little ones,
who'd hardly started their lives
were part of his bloody mystery
when a wave of waste, mud and
slurry, 30 feet high,
ended those lives, drowned the little ones,
just after nine that Friday morning
with half-term starting lunchtime
and days off school to come.

When they got to Heaven, (no
delay getting there
for innocent little ones, straight up
they went)
who knows, maybe He explained it all
to them,
told them why He was being
so mysterious.

But why blame God? It was the fat cats

on the coal board who should have

got the arse-kicking or worse

(but they never did) for piling up

the waste

at the top of the mountain and

knowing it was dangerous

one hundred and ten bloody feet of it,

all just waiting to slide down and drown the village

and kill one hundred and sixteen

little ones,

whose lives had hardly started.

Against the rules it was that high,

but no one cared, why care,

because we're waste, too, see,

we're human waste, human mud

and slurry that don't matter,

human waste who'll dig up their

coal for them

from under the ground

then fuck off when we're told to fuck off

when that's all been done

and they don't need us any more.

Because we don't matter, see,
human waste like us don't count.
Oh, they had a bloody inquiry, led
by some bloody lord
which found the coal board was
certainly to blame.
Well, we knew that, didn't we, but now it was
official, see,
and they even named nine buggers,
nine men who didn't do their bloody job, and
should have known.
But no one got it in the neck, no one,
no one got his arsed kicked and
kicked very bloody hard. No one,
because we're human waste, see,
even the hundred and sixteen little
ones who died.

To show us the kind of shit we were,
they refused to clear the other six tips after,
because of cost, see,
'it's the the cost, dear boy,
it'll cost too much to clear them all,'

they said, it'll cost too much,

so you'll have to live with the other six

because, let's face, you might have lost your little ones

but you're still shit and the money's better spent

on paying the managers a good whack

and making sure there's enough booze in the cupboard

when the board meets.

And shit don't deserve the truth, so

Robens had his minions lie

when they were asked where he was that day,

'Directing the relief work,' they said.

No, he bloody wasn't, his sort don't mix with shit like us

even on a day when one hundred and sixteen of our little ones drown

in a thousand tons of grey waste, mud and slurry.

His lordship was a hundred and sixty miles away,

up in Surrey getting another bloody honour.

But, mate, that was fifty years ago and it
doesn't do to be bitter,

you only poison yourself

and do no harm to any other bugger

however much you want to.

So don't be bitter, don't poison

yourself, butty,

and, no, we're not bitter any more,

we're not,

life is life and death is death,

though no one's yet persuaded us

that if we are shit,

(and maybe we are)

there's another kind of human shit that stinks
even more.

Nothing to say

What, nothing to say?
A generation yet again proclaims
enough is enough is enough!
But you have nothing to say?

Even those unaffected,
whose grandsires were not bought and sold
like cattle, now agree that
enough is enough is enough
and call out to say so.
But you have nothing to say?

They're just thugs who burn and loot?
Yes, certainly, one or two are thugs,
perhaps, though, as balance
to the thugs who oppose
and whose grandsires lynched and killed,
and lynch and kill
and insist that nothing's wrong,
that history was history
that history is history

and there's the end to it.
But you have nothing to say?

You want to keep an open mind?
You drop your pennies
in the box at church,
and kneel in worship,
visit the sick and pray for guidance,
debate the rights and wrongs
of white lies and of this and that,
confess you are a sinner,
just a humble sinner,
and repent
(and bask in your humility).
But still you have nothing to say?

Oh, times were different then?
Were they? Folk did not then love and grieve
and did not dote and weep?
And still we hate, hate as only man can hate,
so not quite as different as you insist.
But you have nothing to say.

The natural order of things?

Yes, of course,

the natural order of things

(though it's odd how only those

who benefit from the natural order of things

will bang that drum.

It's odd how those who suffer from the natural

order of things never do so).

And still you have nothing to say.

You like to keep aloof, above the fray

as all honest brokers must,

if soon to be called upon to forge a peace.

Well, that's one way to go, of course,

and you shine so well in the

gleam and gloss of your cheap honesty.

But let's be frank: you have nothing to say.

Too much, too much

Onomatopoeia?

I don't much like the sound of it.

I really don't.

What is it? What can it be?

Some kind of Japanese cuisine?

An intricate, new, more ethical way of saying
sorry?

Some advanced philosophy that's

all the rage in Paris and New York?

A scalp complaint?

I don't much like the sound of it.

I really don't.

Initial fear

We knew a man who based

it all, his whole philosophy of

life on — what he claimed,

let's get that clear — was

the simple fact requiring nowt but

humour in all, even

in those awkward times and

situations where of necessity

dancing on a pinhead
ought to be enough.
It should be, I know, but isn't that
damn easy to understand and
only those with all the nous available
under the stars dare to
believe for more than a second
that try as we might
it cannot be pulled off
today or any other day

Oh muse, where the fuck are you!

I

So now this.

I had no idea, none,
just none at all. And how could I?

We so rarely speak,
you shout and criticise,
and finally I seem to be a nothing to you,
my concerns, my fears, my thoughts
just brushed away
as irrelevant to our lives.

You say I never listen,
am absent when present,
away somewhere though sitting by your side.

But who can be expected
to cope with your litany of complaint,
the accusations, tears, recrimination,
the eternal headaches, that forever downbeat
air,
an ego so fragile you crave

(well, you craved)
such constant, constant reassurance.
Constant, constant, there was no let-up, none.

And now this.

I had no idea, none,
just none at all. And how could I?

Why did you do it?
Why?
Is your life
(or was your life)
so poor, so miserable and empty,
so meaningless?

So now this.
How can — how could — this solve anything?

And now I am alone,
must face what comes alone,
alone, where once you were there
to share my fears, my concerns, my thoughts.

Oh muse, where the fuck are you!

How could you?
And you accused me
of being the self-centred one
who would destroy you.

How could you?

2020? Who cares

Ten short syllables get my attention
An unobtrusive art defines their role
Repeated hours of careful application
are required to let each find its soul.
As ordained each takes its place in order
No rank or favour, each unique and true,
each does formal duty as demanded
each heralding an old as something new.
This is surely not what you expected
But, unexpected, might yet still delight
A notion noted, then applied, reflected
A poet's whimsy hidden in plain sight.
Now those syllables depart, no longer needed
Their essential role fulfilled and truly heeded.

Oh muse, where the fuck are you!

Plus ça change . . .

When life was still in black and white
We all agreed that we were right
Truth was for the very few
When spoken to we smiled on cue

Nuance was just for gays and dykes
Good friends could be dismissed as kikes
A simper here, a simper there
Could get some jerk out of your hair

Girls knew well to keep it quiet
Don't breathe a word, don't breathe a word
Boys were strong and never cried
And grown-ups never ever lied

Politicos all had our trust
And if one slipped well he was just
The odd one out (a bloody fool
Who'd ignored the simple rule)

We played the game and took great care

Not to notice stinking air

To notice just what was in sight

When life was still in black and white

And now?

Oh muse, where the fuck are you!

I lived and learned

The plan was for us to live together
as we had done when I squatted,
uninvited though not unwelcome,
at your place before you moved away.

We saw each other in turn,
this weekend at mine, that at yours,
but as the day approached for your return
I realised that it was now or never,
the time had come to commit.

And that was when I had my doubts.
I was not young, but still enjoyed
my spliffs too much, the possibility of sex
with other girls (occasionally realised),
and was convinced I was
the apple of your eye.

I still lived far too much in my own self,
taking up most all the space there
and there was barely room for you.

We sat one night with a glass of wine
in a bar near work
chatting of this and that
when I admitted I was unsure
about you moving in
and that perhaps
the time had come to split.

OK, you said. OK.

OK.

It was not what I expected,
not what I hoped for or expected
(though I had and still have
no idea what that might be).

There were no tears, no regret,
no plea to reconsider. There was just OK.

OK.

We went our separate ways

but kept in touch, you without me,
me the one with a regret.

Very, very soon I cursed (and still curse)
my male timidity, my fear, my vanity
my empty certainties.

You later married, I later married
(though not to each other).
But still it's all fresh and sad enough
to be the weave
for a piece of maudlin verse.

That glorious 13th

Freedom? Such a blessed thought.

Jim Crow saw to it that

these are now free:

Breonna, Aura, Atatiana and Botham.

Stephon, Philando, Janisha and Eric.

Alton, Michelle, Akai and Freddie.

Eric, Tamir, Gabriella, Michael and Tanisha.

They might all still get

their forty acres and a mule,

but not in this world.

Ah, freedom, such a blessed thought.

Oh muse, where the fuck are you!

W times five

I don't think you know her,
but I've known her a while now,
but just as friends, though, just as friends,
well, so far, anyway.
Sally Jones (pally Sally, they call her,
she's so bubbly and nice)
and everyone likes her
and she's always helpful
helps everyone, helped me with my essay
so I got quite a good mark for a change.

She kissed me, just like that,
— just like that, right out of the blue,
she suddenly stopped walking,
turned towards me,
pulled my head forward with both hands
and kissed me, a real smacker,
didn't know what to do.
But I didn't mind at all.
And then we carried on walking.

Last night on the way home.
We had a great night with Jo and Joe,
Pete and Linda, Sean and Mandy,
the usual crowd, the usual thing,
a few beers, a game or two of pool,
a lot of laughs,
and then I walked her home,
and then it happened.

Near her flat, down that small lane
by the bus shelter, past the shop, yeah, that's
right,
before the petrol station,
she lives there with her mum.
Been drizzling for a bit, but it had stopped
and everything was lovely, cool and really
fresh,
the clouds were gone,
and the Moon was out, a really lovely night.

Well, I suppose she likes me, got to be.
Got to be. And I like her.
I'm seeing her again, Tuesday,
on our own this time, not with all the others,
We're going for a pizza.

Oh muse, where the fuck are you!

How to live successfully

Life? Simple really,
and don't let the wiseacres
and gurus who say
they want to help you
help yourself
confuse. It's simple,
quite, quite simple.

There are, of course,
the very obvious things —
always wipe your arse
and wash your hands whenever,
but that, in essence, sums it up.

Truth? Only lie
if you really have to,
and if you lie,
keep it simple
and stick to the lie
through thick and thin,
don't vary it (people notice).

Simple, really, that word again.
It's all quite, quite simple

Money?
You can't be clearer
than the man who warned:
don't lend and don't borrow
It always ends in tears,
and the tears are always yours.
If you want something,
save up for it,
bit by bit, a little by little,
and just watch that mountain grow.

The rest of the world?
Treat others as
you would like others
to treat you
except, of course, the bastards,
crap on the bastards, they deserve no better,
(and they know who they are).

And love? Again, it's very simple:
don't fall in love,

Oh muse, where the fuck are you!

it just brings pain.
And don't get too attached,
that's just another straight road
to misery.

Oh, you already are?
You love your partner, friends,
your children, home, your family?

Oh.

Is this poetry?

Is this poetry?
For, to be honest, I have no idea at all
what poetry might be
(unless music plays its part
and that it now does so rarely).

Those of us who know that sound and rhythm,
(the omega and alpha of all that lives and
breathes)
have long known that meaning and
significance
are nothing but a dull and trite subterfuge
lesser muses,
keen to hold their own and not be left behind,
enlist to tarn their conceit,
(and thereby lose for it
all the respect and admiration they crave).

'This is me!' you say, 'but this is me!
Me!' you cry, 'me!'
'Me!'

Well, quite frankly,

we do not give a damn, none of us,

whatever we say.

Your 'me' leaves less time for mine,

for ours.

So by all means tell me your secrets,

Your fears, your woes, the stories of your life
and loves

at great length (if not greater);

and by all means join in the noise,

and add to the cacophony

that bolsters the banalities of life.

But don't — ever — try to persuade me

that yours are more vital and important than

the secrets, noise and banalities

of the one, ten, twenty billion other souls

with whom we share this world.

By all means try, of course: try, why not?

I am polite.

But don't mistake politeness for respect.

Who gets attention? Those who do not crave

it.

So is this poetry?
I don't know.
But I do know it's truth.

Oh muse, where the fuck are you!

Don't cry

At eleven forty of an August morning
she joined us here on Earth,
just one of nine billion
but one in nine billion,
one like no other.

She taught me what it means to love
(but that is by the by,
not I but she is here to cheer your spirit).

One week was an eternity,
then two, then a month,
then one August morning
she had aged a year,
she smiled, she laughed,
she played, she cried,
and soon she walked.

That year became two, then four,
then eight, then twelve
and one night,

as I sat beside her at the supper table,
I saw that this once slip of thing,
once nothing but unwieldy legs and arms
was growing breasts,
small yet, small,
yet significant.

Big school came, and sleepovers
and where-were-you rows
and assurances that no one loved her more
than Mum and I.

At seventeen she left, ostensibly for college
but I knew, though she did not,
that she was leaving for ever.
I did not cry, although I wanted to,
but I did not cry.

She met a boy, a young man,
and went to live with him.
And one day she visited
and told me
'By the way,
you're going to be a granddad'.

Oh muse, where the fuck are you!

And now she has her own one in a billion
And came to learn
and understand
the things
what I had learned
by her simply coming alive
those many years ago.

Men and women

Is it too much to ask that a man,
with his head in his hands,
should shuffle off his festive shroud,
though fecund and fighting fit,
to shrive himself of all
a furtive shame should shoulder;
fighting fit and fecund,
forfeit for ever festivity?

Is that too much to ask?

Must all worldly, wondrous women
behave with the fake worthy winsome
wisdom demanded by the world
to defend their fecund selves before that man,
his head in his hands, has shuffled off
and shriven himself of his furtive shame?

Must they bow yet again, yet once again,
in and to perpetual servitude?

Oh muse, where the fuck are you!

Must they? Must they?

Or shall the world turn as turn it should
to free those finally
whose freedom was always a false favour
to a tribe whose fecund fate it was always
to give way, give way, give way our die?

It must.

It must.

You say her name is what?

You say her name is what? Shriek?
What an odd name! So is it apt?
Does she? Should I avoid her?
Yes, I know, we're due to meet,
her brother set it up, but
he said her name was Anne.

You say it's Shriek? That
doesn't sound like a name I've heard before,
Anne, yes, but Shriek?
What kind of name is that?
Oh, I see, but that's not very nice.

So what shall I do? Ring and say I'm ill?
She'll know it's a lie, she's bound to.
Matter? No, I don't suppose it does,
We don't yet know each other
so what if she does think I'm a heel?
Oh, what the hell, I'll give it a try,
I've nothing else on.

Oh muse, where the fuck are you!

What was it like? Well,
Shriek is rather apt I must admit
and when she laughs! Dear soul!
Yes, Shriek is on the nose.

Coffee with Maria

Bet you a yankee dime, Jose said,
that you can't do it,
bet you can't. I'll give you a day.

Well, I thought,
to refuse when so provoked
would be a crime,
but at first and at last it seemed
more likely that he'd win.

I'm no good at this, I thought
but in time the very obvious words
did occur to me
but none would, could or should
chime as it might with the original
in the spirit of my task.

Which ones?
Lime? OK, yes, perhaps,
but like all the others
perhaps still too obvious

Oh muse, where the fuck are you!

and so a word that would
barely survive any nuance test.

I slept on it and woke to cold and a frost
the world covered in a slight
rime (and don't think
that irony did not hit home)

Later, across the street from her balcony
to me on mine, Maria began
her almost daily mime
of putting to her lips a virtual cup
and drinking. Coffee? Now?
Anything, I thought, anything.

We met at Silvio's and I told her
how I was about to lose a bet.
Who cares, she said, who cares.
You men, she said, you men,
you lose yourselves in triviality
and don't notice that the world
is moving on.
Who cares.

But I do, I thought, I do, I care.
though I didn't tell her and risk
her further woman's scorn
(too much for any man to bear).

Ah, Jose would understand
when I told him I'd failed.
He was a fellow man,
and though he would crow, boast
and remind I had lost
and he had won,
he would, at least, understand.

So much for coffee with Maria.

Oh muse, where the fuck are you!

Don't push your luck

Please! Don't badger me!
Let's get that straight!
There's more than one way
to catch a fly
and you'll catch more with sugar
than with a saucer full
of your sour vinegar.
Bear that in mind, please, always,
— always — and we might stay friends.

So what's it you want?
You've been banging on so long
I really can't remember what.
What was it?
You want me to agree?
Agree to what?
Nothing, I hope,
I'll later regret,
so tell me.

Oh, that? All right, it's a yes.

But now I've said yes,

that's the last I want to hear of it,

and if I do

I might not quite be so amenable.

How to succeed

Use rhyme, dear boy, use rhyme
and then in time,
when you've used rhyme
the time will come
when rhyme is no longer necessary,
when those you hoped in time,
by using rhyme,
to impress, subdue, inoculate and dazzle,
will agree — and they will!
— agree among themselves,
in quiet and wistful
(and quite envious) gatherings
(by email, phone or even post)
that, yes, the lad has talent,
good lord but does the lad have talent!
and, yes, good lord! but does the lad quite
simply know
what it is and how
to sparkle, sparkle, sparkle
subdue, impress and inoculate himself
against the undue, unfair, unwise and quite
unwarranted cynicism that it's all just a pose,

all nothing but an act, that
all that supposed poetry
is just a mealy posturing, an overflow of vanity
and nothing — nothing! — more.

Avoid all that, dear boy, avoid all that
by using rhyme.

Oh muse, where the fuck are you!

2020? Who cares?

Ten short syllables get my attention
An unobtrusive art defines their role
Repeated hours of careful application
are required to let each find its soul.
As ordained each takes its place in order
No rank or favour, each unique and true,
each does formal duty as demanded
each heralding an old as something new.
This is surely not what you expected
But, unexpected, might yet still delight
A notion noted, then applied, reflected
A poet's whimsy hidden in plain sight.
Now those syllables depart, no longer needed
Their essential role fulfilled and truly heeded.

Default setting

I thought for many years
that we might reach some kind of
understanding,
some way of living,
some escape from our sad and dull routine
of argument and shouts,
of day-long silences,
of miserable meals when nothing is said
(or so very little
— 'would you pass the salt?
Thank you.'
— 'Ask your father
if he wants a cup of tea.')

I thought we might grow,
grow together, grow up,
mature,
put behind us our late middle-aged adolescent
urge
to best the other,
to win, to win,
to own that last word

Oh muse, where the fuck are you!

(which was never owned by you or I
never the last but always trumped).

I hoped that our love for our children,
our fear and concern
(we talked about it so many times
when we tried to sort out our love)
that letting them live, soak up and grow
in noise and anger
would not let them see
that ours was not the only way,
that our angry home was not
the only kind of home,
that some families did know a steady peace
and love.

And then they left and now are gone,
beyond our love and concern.

And then you died,
long, long, long before it was expected.
So now there can be no change, no
compromise
no steady peace and love.

Now it no longer is
but was.

Oh muse, where the fuck are you!

Oh muse, where the fuck are you!

Oh muse, where the fuck are you!

Printed in Great Britain
by Amazon